Famou Illustrated Tales of AKBAR & BIRBAL

MAPLE KIDS

Famous Illustrated Tales of
AKBAR & BIRBAL

Published by

MAPLE PRESS PRIVATE LIMITED

Corporate & Editorial Office
A 63, Sector 58, Noida 201 301, U.P., India

phone: +91 120 455 3581, 455 3583
email: info@maplepress.co.in
website: www.maplepress.co.in

Printed in 2022

ISBN: 978-93-50339-07-7

Authors: Poonam Mittal & Saurabh Mittal
Printed at Diamond Agencies Private Limited, Noida, India

14 13 12 11 10 9 8 7 6 5

Contents

Sharing of Reward

Emperor Akbar was very fond of learned and gifted men. Often when a gifted man would come to the emperor, he would appoint the man as one of his ministers. Akbar's court was full of intelligent and wise men. Out of them, nine men were known as the nine gems of Akbar's court. They were exceptionally talented and accomplished men in their fields.

Once, a young man called Mahesh Das lived in a small village in Akbar's kingdom. Since he had spent his entire young life in this village, he now wished to travel the world. He had heard many stories about the big city and the emperor's palace. It sounded like an exciting place to be in and he decided to pay the emperor a visit and see if he could get a job.

He travelled through many crowded bazaars and towns. Finally, he reached the city. Mahesh Das went up to the palace gate. But he could not enter. The gatekeeper caught him. He asked, "Where do you think you are going?"

Mahesh Das replied, "I am going to see the emperor." The guard burst out laughing. "He has personally invited you to have dinner with him in his dining chamber I suppose," the guard said. Mahesh Das remained quiet. The guard continued,

"It is not possible for you to see the king. He is a very busy man. I have orders from the king not to let anybody in."

Mahesh Das pleaded with the guard to let him in. The guard said, "I told you I can't let you in." Mahesh Das said, "But why?" The guard said, "Because you are poor. Everyone whom I allow to see the emperor pays me something like a cow, a goat or embroidered slippers. What can you give me?"

Mahesh Das said, "I don't have anything now. But I can promise you that I will give you half of what I get from the emperor as a reward." The guard knew the emperor was a generous one. He often gave expensive gifts to people who came to see him. So the guard quickly agreed.

Mahesh Das entered the palace. He was amazed by the richly embroidered golden curtains and carpets. The palace was made of red sandstone and was lavishly decorated. Emperor Akbar sat at the middle of the court. Mahesh Das bowed to Akbar. Akbar said, "I am very pleased with the respect you have shown me. What do you want from me in return?" Mahesh Das said, "*Jahanpanah*, if I may, I shall ask that you grant that I may receive one hundred lashes on my bare back."

The emperor was surprised. He said, "That is a very strange request. Why do you want me to give you hundred lashes?" Mahesh Das said,

"Your majesty, when I was coming to see you, the gatekeeper told me to give him half of what I get from you."

Akbar laughed. Then he said, "This is a serious issue. This means the gatekeeper accepts bribes for doing his job. He should be punished."

The gatekeeper was brought in and given hundred lashes as a punishment for accepting bribes. Then Akbar said to Mahesh Das, "You are a very clever man. Why don't you stay at my court as my minister?" Mahesh Das was happy to accept the offer. From that day, he came to be known as Birbal as stories of his wit became famous far and wide.

The Fake Lion

The emperor of Persia and Emperor Akbar were very good friends. They would often send jokes and riddles to each other. It helped them to maintain a good friendship as they enjoyed receiving parcels from each other.

One day Akbar received a large cage from the emperor of Persia with a fake lion inside and a letter. The letter said, "If there be a wise man in your court he should take out the lion without opening the cage. If the cage could not be emptied the Mughal territories would come under the sovereignty of the emperor of Persia."

Akbar cast an anxious glance over all his courtiers one by one, then said, "I know all of you are learned, intelligent and expert in your fields. Can anyone take out the lion without opening the cage. Can anyone do it?"

He again looked at his courtiers expectantly. Everyone sat frozen in their seats. All of them looked amazed and embarrassed as if it was beyond their understanding. They were looking at each other. They disappointed the emperor.

That day, Birbal was absent in the court. He was engaged in some official work elsewhere. Akbar wished Birbal had been there in the court at that moment. He ordered his messengers to look for Birbal.

The next day Akbar was sitting on his throne rather relaxed. All the seats were occupied by the courtiers. One was unoccupied as Birbal hadn't yet arrived. Then Birbal entered the court. He bowed and said, "*Jahanpanah*! I am here present in your service. What are the orders for me?"

Akbar briefly told him the whole matter and handed him the Persian emperor's letter. Birbal read the letter and cast an eyeful glance at the cage.

Birbal called a servant and ordered a heated iron rod to be brought. The servant instantly obeyed. Birbal touched the lion with the heated iron rod. The lion melted slightly at that place. He continued touching until the whole lion melted.

The Persian courtier was greatly impressed by Birbal's brilliance. Akbar asked, "How did you know that the lion was made up of wax."

"*Huzoor*," replied Birbal, "According to the letter the cage was to be emptied without opening it. It said nothing about the lion being kept intact. I just tried an idea that it might be made of wax."

The Persian courtier returned to his country to tell one more story of Birbal's brilliance.

Turns in a Street

Once, the emperor of Persia sent Akbar a strange letter. In that letter he asked Akbar to tell him how many turns each street in his kingdom had. Akbar was shocked by the question. His kingdom was a large one. How would it be possible for him to send his ministers to count the number of turns in all the streets?

Nevertheless, the emperor called his prime minister, Todarmal and asked him to take the project. Todarmal in return sent his men to count the number of turns all the streets in the kingdom had.

Next day Birbal noticed that Akbar was waiting anxiously for something. Birbal asked, "*Jahanpanah*, is there something wrong? You look so much worried."

Akbar said, "Yes, Birbal I am waiting for Todarmal to report the number of turns all the streets in my kingdom had." He then told Birbal about the letter that the emperor of Persia had sent him.

When Birbal heard of it he laughed out loudly. Akbar was puzzled when he saw Birbal laughing. Birbal said, "Your majesty, I know the exact number of

turns of each street not only in our kingdom but in any city of the world."

Akbar's eyes grew wide. He said, "I hope you are not joking. I have sent so many men to count the number of turns and here you say you know it already?"

Birbal said, "I am not joking my lord. All the streets of the world have only two turns, a left turn and a right turn." At this the emperor burst out laughing. It was an easy answer and he had not thought of it. He rewarded Birbal handsomely and called the royal poet to send the reply to the emperor of Persia.

The Real Mother

As the 'shadow of God on earth', so it was the emperor's duty to establish peace and order in his kingdom by protecting the weak and punishing the wicked. Akbar took pride in his fairness. After all he was *jahanpanah*, the refuge of the world.

One day in his royal court came two women with a little boy. Both of them were crying bitterly.

The first woman said, "*Jahanpanah*, this little boy is my son. I had left him with my friend because I was very sick and I could not take care of him. But now when I am well again, she is refusing to give my son back to me."

At this the second woman wailed before the *sultan*, "She is a liar, my lord. This is my son. I am his mother. This woman wants to take my son away; that is why she is telling you such stories."

Akbar could not decide how to bring justice to the women. He called his most wise minister Birbal to the court. Birbal listened to both the women one by one and nodded his head. Then he bowed to Akbar and said, "*Jahanpanah*, both of these women claim to be the mother of the child. So it is best that we give the child to both of them." The court including the *sultan* looked at Birbal in surprise. Birbal continued, "Let us cut the child into two

equal halves and give each part to each woman. That way both shall have the child."

Birbal asked the guard to take the child to the royal butcher and have him cut into two halves. The guard took the child by his arm when the first woman wailed and fell at the *sultan's* feet. She begged, "Mercy my lord, do not harm my child. Let the second woman keep him. I withdraw my complaint. I love my child. I cannot bear to see any harm done to him."

Birbal smiled and said to Akbar, "Your majesty, this is the real mother of the child. A mother will bear anything but she cannot bear to see her child come to any harm."

Everyone present at the court applauded Birbal's wit. Akbar gave Birbal a handsome reward for solving the problem.

The Magic Sticks

Once upon a time there lived a rich oil merchant in the great city of Fatepur Sikri. He had gifted a diamond necklace to his wife which made her very happy. The necklace was very costly and the woman loved it very much. She would often wear it to attend the parties and special occasions when her friends came to visit her. So the necklace became famous as many women admired it.

But one day when the wife woke up in the morning, she could not find the necklace anymore. She searched and searched for it but the necklace could not be seen anywhere. Thus, it was concluded that the necklace had been stolen.

The merchant sent his guards to find out who had stolen it. Then the guards searched for the thief but whoever had stolen it was very clever. He had left no clue for the guards. The guards could not find out who had stolen the necklace. It made the wife very sad.

The merchant began to worry about his wife's health. Left with

no option, he called upon Birbal to solve the case. Birbal was a good friend of the merchant's. One day, he came over for dinner. He said, "The diamond necklace was in the lady's cupboard at all times. It was stolen; it must be done by some of your servants. Call all your servants here. I must talk to them."

The servants were called to the dining hall. Birbal said to the servants, "I have some magic sticks here. I will give two sticks to each of you. Give it back to me tomorrow."

One of the servants said, "But how would you find out who is the thief by using these sticks?"

Birbal said, "These are no ordinary sticks. The sticks of the thief will grow two inches overnight. So when I measure all your sticks tomorrow, I will know who the thief is."

The merchant was surprised but he did not say anything. The next day the servants brought back the sticks to Birbal. Birbal measured the sticks, one by one and said to the merchant, "Your cook is your thief."

Everyone was surprised. The merchant said, "How can you say that?" Birbal replied, "The sticks I gave him are short by two inches. He thought that since he is the thief, the stick would grow by two inches. So he has cut them two inches so as not to get caught."

The merchant laughed. The cook had to give the necklace back and he lost his job. Everyone praised Birbal for his intelligence.

Owner of the Money Bag

Once in the city of Agra, there lived a butcher. He was an honest man who never set high price or adulterated the meat he sold. So he had many customers for he sold the finest meat in the city. Everyone in the city knew about his shop and they often recommended the shop to their friends and family. On festivals his shop would be flooded by people and the butcher would be busy all day serving them.

On one such a day a grain merchant came to the butcher's shop. The butcher was counting his money then. The merchant asked for a kg of meat. The butcher placed his money bag on the counter and left to get the meat from the store. But when he returned, he was surprised. He saw that the money bag was now with the merchant and he was paying for the meat from it. The butcher was very angry. He said, "Excuse me sir, I think you have stolen my money bag. I had left it on the counter before I went to get the meat."

The merchant said, "How dare you call me a thief? This is my money bag. I brought it with me to the shop."

The butcher said, "How can I believe you have not taken my bag from the counter?" The merchant replied, "How can I believe you had left your bag on

the counter? You might be making it up so that I am forced to give my bag to you."

A fight broke out between the butcher and the merchant. Many people gathered around them. Finally, someone suggested that they went to Birbal. He would find a way of solving this problem. So the merchant and the butcher went to Birbal.

Birbal carefully studied the money bag. Then he asked the merchant, "Do you deal in blood?" The merchant was puzzled. He said, "No sir, I deal in grains. I am scared of blood so much that it makes me feel dizzy. I try to stay away from it as much as possible." Birbal smiled and handed the bag to the butcher. Birbal said, "The bag has blood stains on it. Some of the coins are also stained with blood. If you are so afraid of blood the bag can't belong to you. Can it?"

The merchant was punished for stealing. The butcher thanked Birbal and went back to his shop, happily.

Dishonest Judge

Akbar's kingdom was very large. So he appointed judges who would help the people who faced various problems in the city.

One day a woman went to one such judge with a bag of gold coins. She said, "Sir, this is my life's savings. I am going on a pilgrimage and I can't carry so much money with me. Please keep this bag safely with you until I return."

The judge kept the bag and bade farewell to the woman. After a month the woman returned. She went straight to the judge and collected the bag. But when she went home and removed the seal, she saw that the bag contained flat stones. Her gold coins had vanished.

She went to the judge and started arguing. The judge said, "Wicked woman. You had filled stones in the bag and now you want me to pay you?" She had no other way. She ran to the emperor's court for justice.

When Akbar heard her story, he was puzzled. The judge was an old and powerful man. Akbar could not punish him without a witness. So he called Birbal and explained everything to him. Birbal thought for a while and said to the emperor, "My lord, tear your bed

sheet today before you go to bed. I shall solve the case tomorrow."

The next day, Akbar told Birbal that he had done exactly as Birbal had asked him to but before he got up he saw that the bed sheet was like new again. Birbal smiled and said, "*Jahanpanah*, give me ten minutes, I will bring your witness to you." After ten minutes Birbal brought an old tailor to the court. The tailor said, "Yes, your majesty. The old judge had brought a bag for me to sew. I didn't understand why he needed to put flat stones in it before having it sewn."

The woman brought out the bag and asked the tailor, "Was this the bag?" The tailor nodded.

Akbar called for the judge and asked him to return the money. He then ordered fifty lashes to be given to the judge for cheating.

Akbar asked Birbal, how he found out about the tailor. Birbal said, "My lord, when you said that your bed sheet was as good as new in the morning, I asked the maid who cleaned your room about the tailor she had gone to get the bed sheet stitched. I found that this old man was the only tailor in the city who could stitch and make the thing as good as new. So I guessed he must have stitched the bag of coins which the judge had ripped apart to take the coins out."

Akbar praised Birbal's wisdom when he heard this story.

Miser Merchant

In Akbar's kingdom lived a man called Harinath. Harinath was a gifted painter. He would make portraits and earn his living. Because he was very good at making portraits, he was very popular in the city. Rich people from far and wide would request him to make portraits for them. But Harinath would take a long time to make a portrait for he was very careful with the details. Thus, though his portraits were very life-like, he could not earn enough money for them. Also the money earned would go into buying of raw materials for the paintings.

One day a very rich merchant invited Harinath to make a portrait of him. Harinath went to the merchant's house hoping that he will be paid well for his work. He stayed there for days, working hard to satisfy the merchant with the painting.

But the merchant was a miser. When after days of hard work the portrait was complete Harinath brought it to the merchant.

But the miserly merchant thought to himself, "This painting is indeed very good. But if I appreciate its beauty, I will have to pay hundred gold coins to Harinath." So the merchant began to find faults with it. He said, "You have shown grey hair and made me look like an old man. I am not going to pay you."

Harinath was surprised for he did not know that the merchant was finding faults with the painting so that he would not have to pay Harinath. Harinath said, "My lord, I will retouch the painting if you want." So he worked at covering all the grey hair in the portrait. But when the merchant saw the painting after the retouching he found more faults with it. He said, "One of my eyes is smaller than the other. I will not pay you for this rubbish."

Harinath offered to retouch the painting further. This went on for quite some days. Every time Harinath took the painting to the merchant he found more faults with it. Finally, Harinath grew tired of the merchant. He went to Birbal for help.

Birbal asked Harinath to invite the merchant to Birbal's house. Birbal said to the merchant, "This man says he had drawn a life-like portrait for you exactly the way you wanted, but you did not like it."

The merchant said, "That's correct my lord. The portrait did not look like me at all."

Birbal said, "Fine. Harinath, make another portrait of this man and make it look exactly like him." He then turned to the merchant and said, "Please come and collect it tomorrow. But you will have to pay one thousand gold coins for it because I will be watching Harinath while he makes it so that there are no faults." The merchant thought, a portrait made in a day will have many faults. I will not have to work hard to find those faults.

Next day when he came, Birbal took the merchant to a room. A portrait stood in the room. It was covered by a cloth. When the merchant removed the cloth he was astonished. It was not a portrait at all, but a mirror. Birbal said, "This looks exactly like you, doesn't it? I hope you will not find any faults with it."

The merchant realized that Birbal had won. He had to pay the hundred gold coins for the portrait as well as one thousand gold coins for the mirror.

Birbal's Journey to Heaven

When Birbal joined Akbar's court, some of the ministers at Akbar's court were not happy. Akbar had begun to favour Birbal more. This made the ministers very jealous of Birbal. They decided to take the help of the royal barber.

The barber was a poor man. The ministers presented him with a bag of gold which he could not resist. So he agreed to help. One day as he was giving the emperor a hair cut he said, "*Jahanpanah*, I had a dream last night. Your father came in my dream and said that he was doing well in heaven. He has asked you not to worry."

The emperor became sad when he heard this. His father had died when he was very young.

He asked, "What else did my father say. Tell me everything." The barber said, "*Jahanpanah*, he said that he was fine, only a bit bored. He said, if you could send Birbal to him, it would make him very happy. He watches Birbal from the heaven and praises him for his wit and humour."

Akbar called for Birbal at once. He said, "Dear Birbal, I am really very fond of you. So it makes me very sad to send you to my father who is in heaven. But he has asked for you. You must go to heaven and entertain him."

Birbal was very shocked when he heard this. Later he

learnt the servants that it was a plan by the minister and the barber. He dug a grave near his home and from the grave he dug a tunnel which led to his living room. Then he went to Akbar and said, "Your majesty, I am ready to go to heaven. But we have a family tradition that we are all buried outside our home. I have already arranged for the grave. I request you to have me buried alive there."

Akbar granted Birbal's wish. Birbal was buried alive. He escaped from the grave through the tunnel and came home. After three weeks he went to Akbar's court. Everyone was surprised to see Birbal. Akbar said, "When did you come back from the heaven? How is my father? And why do you look so shabby?"

Birbal said, "My lord, your father is fine. He has sent you his blessings. But *jahanpanah*, there are no barbers in heaven. That's why I look so shabby. If you would be kind to send the royal barber to your father it would make him very happy."

The emperor at once ordered the barber to be buried alive and sent to heaven. The barber fell at Akbar's feet and begged, "Oh no, I don't want to die! I don't want to die! I was tricked into this wicked plan." He confessed everything.

Akbar banished all the ministers who tried to trick Akbar into killing his favourite minister. The barber got ten lashes as a punishment. As for Birbal, he continued to live in the court as the emperor's advisor and closest friend.

Story of a Smart Cheat

Once there lived a man in Akbar's city. He had a very strange way of making a living. He would cheat people and made them pay him a lot of money. One day, he met a very rich merchant at the market. The merchant had travelled from a foreign country. He was new in the city. So when the cheat invited him to his house for dinner, the merchant accepted it hoping to make some friends in the new city.

That night, they had a delicious dinner and talked for a long time. Then the merchant and his host went to bed. Next morning, the cheat said to the merchant, "I had invited you to dinner. I played such a good host and this is how you have paid me back?"

The merchant was totally confused. He said, "I don't know what you are talking about!" The cheat said, "You have stolen my diamond. I want it back!" The merchant said, "Friend, I don't know what diamond you are talking about. I have absolutely no idea."

They began to fight. Finally, they decided to go to the court to sort it out.

Emperor Akbar was puzzled when he heard both their stories. He asked Birbal to solve the case.

The cheat said, "*Jahanpanah*, I have witnesses who have seen the merchant stealing my diamond." Birbal said, "Please call upon your witnesses. I would like to ask them about it."

A barber and a tailor were the cheat's witnesses. Birbal gave each of them a lump of clay and asked them to shape it as a diamond. They were taken to different rooms to work on the clay.

The barber had never seen a diamond in his life. His father told him that to a barber a razor was what a diamond was to a diamond merchant. He molded the clay into a razor.

The tailor's mother too, had told him that a needle must mean to a tailor the way a diamond means to a diamond merchant. He molded the clay in the shape of a needle.

When Birbal saw what the witnesses had made, he said, "*Jahanpanah*, none of these men have ever seen a diamond, so how could they have seen the merchant steal the diamond? The story is a lie. The merchant is innocent."

It was proven that the cheat had bribed the barber and the tailor to be false witnesses. He was jailed for cheating, while the merchant happily went back home.

Counting of Crows

Once a very famous scholar had travelled from the neighbouring kingdom to Akbar's court. The man bowed to the emperor and said, "*Jahanpanah*, I have heard a lot about Birbal's intelligence. People from far and wide often enjoy the stories about his wit. Your highness, if you allow, I would like to test his talent."

Akbar called upon Birbal and introduced him to the scholar. The scholar said, "Tell me how many crows live in your city?"

Birbal heard the question calmly and said, "My friend, I shall surely give you the answer tomorrow." Everyone at the court was surprised at the conversation between the scholar and Birbal. Emperor Akbar called Birbal aside and asked, "This man seems to be mad. How is it possible for a person to count the number of crows living in this city? It will take days before you find the right answer. You will never be able to count all of them in a day."

Birbal smiled and said, "*Jahanpanah*, this man is trying to outsmart me. But do not worry. He will get the taste of his own medicine."

Next day Birbal came to the court. The scholar was already seated there. The scholar said, "Have

you found out the answer?" Birbal said, "Of course. There are exactly forty seven thousand eight hundred and thirty five crows in this city."

The scholar was very surprised at the answer. He said, "How can you be so sure?" Birbal bowed to Akbar and said, "*Jahanpanah*, I have counted all the crows in this city including the ones that have migrated from the neighbouring kingdoms. If anyone doubts my answer, it is only fitting that he should count them himself for his satisfaction."

Akbar burst out laughing. The scholar was very ashamed of himself when he heard Birbal. He left the city that day itself promising that he would never challenge anyone again.

Birbal and Three Dolls

O nce, a very famous artist came to Akbar's court carrying three beautiful dolls. The dolls looked exactly same. They were so similar that it was difficult to tell the difference between them. Akbar loved the dolls. He said, "Sell me the dolls and I will give you a handsome price."

The artist said, "*Jahanpanah*, these dolls are not for sale. However, I shall give them to you as a gift if anyone from your court can tell which of the three dolls is the best."

This was a strange puzzle. Akbar took the dolls and looked at them closely. But the three dolls were so similar that Akbar could not say which was the best. Then each of his ministers tried to solve the puzzle but they failed.

Akbar called Birbal, "Dear Birbal, why don't you try? I am sure you will be able to solve the puzzle." Birbal bowed to Akbar and went up to the dolls. He took each doll in his hand. He observed them very closely. Then to everyone's astonishment, he blew into one doll's ear. The wind came out of its other ear. Then he blew into another doll's ear. This time the wind came out

of its mouth. When Birbal blew into the third doll's ear, the wind did not come out at all.

Birbal said, "*Jahanpanah*, the third doll is the best out of the three." Akbar was surprised. He said, "How did you know that?" Birbal said, "My lord, the three dolls are like three kinds of men. When I blew into the ear of the first doll, the wind came out of its other ear. Just as when we tell a secret to some men, they forget it the next minute. When I blew into the second doll's ear, the wind came out of its mouth just as some men who speak out what they have heard. Such men cannot keep a secret. But when I blew into the ear of the third doll, the wind did not come out at all. These kinds of men are best for they can keep a secret. You can tell them about any secret matter."

The artist said, "I had only heard about Birbal's wisdom, but today I have seen it too. *Jahanpanah*, these dolls are yours."

Akbar said, he was very proud of Birbal.

Mother Tongue

Once, a strange man came to Akbar's court and bowed respectfully to the emperor. He said, "*Jahanpanah*, I can speak many different languages. I can be of great service to you if you let me stay in your court as one of your ministers."

Emperor decided to test the strange man. He asked his ministers to speak to the man in different languages. In Akbar's court, there were people from many different parts of India. All of them spoke different languages. Each minister came forward and spoke to the man to which the man replied in the same language. Everyone praised the man for his skill with languages.

Akbar was very impressed. He offered the man to be his minister. But the man said, "Your majesty, I have spoken in many different languages today. Can anyone in your court tell what my mother tongue is?"

Many ministers tried guessing his mother tongue. But they failed. The man began to laugh at the ministers. He said, "I have heard that the ministers here are the best brains of the kingdom. But I think I was wrongly told."

The emperor was embarrassed. He looked around for Birbal for help. He said to Birbal, "Please do something to save me from such humiliation."

Birbal said to the man, " My friend, you look tired.

You must have travelled a long distance to come to the court. Please rest for today. I shall answer your question tomorrow morning." Indeed, the man was tired. He took the emperor's leave and left to have some dinner. He was given a warm welcome by the emperor. He had a delicious dinner after which he was taken to the royal guest room where he went to bed.

After all the ministers had left, Akbar asked Birbal, "How will you be able to answer the man's question?" Birbal said, "*Jahanpanah*, do not worry. I have a plan."

That night when everyone in the palace was fast asleep, Birbal wrapped a black shawl around himself and quietly crept into the strange man's room. With a twig of hay, Birbal tickled the man's ears. The man soon woke up. But when he saw a black figure in the dark he thought he had seen a ghost. He screamed and began to shout in Oriya language, "Oh lord *Jagannath*, save me! I have been attacked by a ghost!"

Suddenly the emperor entered the room along with his ministers. Birbal threw the shawl on the floor and lit the lights. He said to man, "So, you are from Orissa and your mother tongue is Oriya. Am I right?" The man realized that Birbal had very cleverly tricked him. He told Birbal that he was right.

Akbar said, "A man can speak many different languages but he will always scream in his mother tongue when he is scared." Birbal had solved the puzzle and the emperor praised him for his cleverness.

A Matter of Devotion

Emperor Akbar was well known for his love of arts and religion. One of the arts that he was fond of, was music, and just like Birbal who was considered as one of the nine jewels of King Akbar's court, Tansen was one of the jewels greatly known and respected for his singing. It is said that there was none better than Tansen for no one could compete with him when it came to singing.

Once, Akbar was much pleased with Tansen's music. He praised Tansen. He said to Tansen, "You are the best artist in the world. Your music is so great that it has no comparison."

Tansen was overwhelmed with gratitude. But he was a simple man. He said, "Your majesty, this is only your opinion. There are artists in the world, who are better than me."

Akbar said, "Come now Tansen, you are being modest. I have heard many singers. But your music is the best amongst all of them."

Tansen said, "Then your majesty, you must listen to my master, Guru Swami Haridas. He is way better than I am. His music is really very beautiful."

Akbar was curious. He said, "Is it so? Then I must hear your *guru* sing. Surely you can request him to sing for me."

Tansen said, "Your majesty, Swami Haridas

would never come to the court and sing for you. But if you come with me to his house, you can hear him sing." Akbar was very eager to listen to Swami Haridas sing. He agreed at once and along with his favourite minister Birbal and Tansen, he reached Swami Haridas' house.

Akbar stayed at Swami Haridas' house for couple of days but the *guru* never sang. Akbar was getting impatient. He called Tansen and asked, "When will Swami Haridas sing? I have been here for four days now but he has not sung a syllable. If this goes on I would have to return to the palace without having heard him sing."

Tansen said, "My lord, *guruji* would sing only when he thinks the time is right. We must have patience."

Then one morning Akbar was woken from his sleep by a very melodious voice. Swami Haridas was singing. His voice was so deep and beautiful that the emperor was mesmerized completely. He said to Tansen, "You were right. Indeed Swami Haridas is better than you." Tansen bowed to the emperor.

Akbar decided to return to the palace now. He felt very satisfied after hearing Swami Haridas sing. On the way back, he asked Birbal, "Birbal, Swami Haridas is a brilliant singer. Why is Tansen's music not so good as his master's?"

Birbal said, "*Jahanpanah*, it is because Tansen sings to please you. But Swami Haridas sings to please God. It is a matter of devotion." Akbar remained silent until they safely reached the palace.

God Saves His Devotees

Though Akbar was a Muslim ruler, he respected all religions equally and was ever curious to know more about God. One day he asked Birbal, "Birbal, is it true that one of Gods in Hindu mythology rushed to rescue an elephant who prayed to him for help?"

Birbal said, "Yes, my lord. When Gajendra the king of elephant's was grabbed by a crocodile who wanted to kill him, he prayed to lord Vishnu. Lord Vishnu answered his prayers and he came to Gajendra's rescue."

Akbar said, "Why did God come to rescue Gajendra himself. He could have sent his servants. He has many servants, doesn't he?"

Birbal said, "I shall answer this question in a few days."

The prince would often go for walks in the evening with his servant. Birbal cleverly befriended the servant and asked him not to tell anyone that they were friends. Then he got a wax statue made, which looked exactly like the prince. One evening when the prince was sleeping, Birbal asked the servant to take the statue for a walk instead of the prince. The servant did as he was told.

Soon after the servant came running to Akbar saying, "*Jahanpanah*, come quickly, the prince has

fallen into the pond. He does not know how to swim."

When Akbar heard this he leapt from his throne at once and ran towards the pond. When he reached the pond he jumped into it to rescue the prince. Akbar was very relieved when he did not find the prince in the pond. Instead, he found the statue which looked like the prince. Birbal was waiting for the emperor to come out of the water.

Akbar asked Birbal, "What kind of joke was this?" Birbal said, "*Jahanpanah*, why did you jump into the pond yourself? You could have sent a servant to save the prince. You have many servants, don't you?"

Akbar remembered the question about God he had asked Birbal. Birbal continued. "God loves his devotees in the same way as you love your son. It is because of this love that he himself rushes to rescue them. The other day you inquired why lord Vishnu himself went to rescue Gajendra from a crocodile. Now you have the answer."

Akbar said, "No one could have explained it to me better. I understand now."

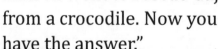

Greater than God

One day Emperor Akbar had invited some close friends over for dinner. Birbal was also there. Many delicious dishes were served and the party enjoyed it very much.

After dinner the guests requested to be entertained. A famous storyteller was called. He began to tell funny stories. Akbar and his guests laughed heartily at the stories. Akbar was so happy with the story teller that he offered the man a bag of gold coins. Indeed, the emperor loved to hear stories and this man was very good at telling stories.

The man was very pleased at the emperor's gesture. He took the bag of gold from the emperor and bowed respectfully. Then he said, "You are the greatest king that ever was. In fact, you are greater than the God."

No sooner had the man said this, there was a silence in the court. The ministers thought, "Greater than God? How can a man be greater than God?" Akbar was very pleased to hear what the story teller had said. Though he too knew

that the storyteller had gone a little overboard with the praise, he found it very funny to see the surprised faces around him. He decided to have some fun.

When the storyteller had left, the emperor turned around to his guests and ministers and asked, "Do you agree with what the man just said? Do you think I am greater than God?"

The guests and the ministers remained quiet. They did not know what to say. Surely, the emperor was not greater than God. But to say that would offend the emperor and he might punish them. Akbar kept teasing them. He said, "I am happy you think I am greater than God. Now tell me why am I greater than God?"

The guests and ministers looked at each other. They were truly lost for words. Akbar looked at Birbal. He said, "Tell me Birbal, why do you think I am greater than God?"

Birbal said, "*Jahanpanah*, you can do something which God cannot. You can banish a wicked man from your kingdom. God cannot do so. Since he owns the universe, where could he send the man? So you are greater than God."

Akbar burst out laughing. Even he had not thought of such an answer. He said, "Dear Birbal, your wit has no match." The guests and the minister heaved a sigh of relief. They took laughed at Birbal's answer.

Unlucky Face

Once there lived a young man in Akbar's city. He had no friends for people hated him. They would make fun of him and throw stones at him whenever he was out in the streets. Yusuf's life was miserable, for everyone thought that he was unlucky. People would say that a glance at Yusuf's face would bring bad luck to the person.

Thus, even though Yusuf was hated, his story was famous far and wide. The rumours reached Akbar's ears. He wanted to test if what people said was true. He invited Yusuf to the court and spoke to him politely. But just then a messenger came running to the court and informed Akbar that the queen had taken seriously ill. The messenger said, "*Jahanpanah*, you are requested at the queen's chambers urgently. The queen has fainted and the physicians are unable to understand why."

Akbar rushed to his queen. He sat by her bed all afternoon. When the queen was feeling better again in the evening, Akbar returned to the court. Yusuf was still waiting for him.

But on seeing Yusuf, Akbar got very angry. He roared, "So the rumours are true. You are indeed unlucky. You have made the queen ill." He ordered the prison guards to take Yusuf away.

Poor Yusuf had no option. He wailed aloud and

begged the guards to let him be free. The decision of the emperor was so unfair. But no one at the court dared to say anything in protest for they feared the emperor.

Suddenly Birbal walked to where Yusuf was standing and whispered something in his ear. Yusuf bowed to the king and said, "*Jahanpanah*, I am ready to go to prison, but after you have answered my humble question. If the queen is ill because you saw my face, then is it not possible that I am being sent to prison because I saw your face?"

Akbar realized his mistake. He let Yusuf go and granted him a bag of gold from the treasury. Once again, the people in the court praised Birbal's wisdom and intelligence.

Birbal's Cooking of Khichdi

Akbar's city of Fatepur Sikhri would get very cold during winters. Once, the emperor announced that he would give a thousand gold coins to anyone who would dare to stand all night in the cold lake just outside the royal palace.

For many days, Akbar received no volunteers. Then one day a poor *brahmin* came to the court. The emperor was amazed when he saw the poor man. He was thin and sickly. The emperor asked, "You are so thin and sickly. Why do you want to take up this difficult challenge?"

The *brahmin* said, "My lord, I am a poor man. I have little children to feed. I need the money."

Akbar agreed and the *brahmin* was led to the lake by two guards. The *brahmin* took off his clothes, stepped into the water and stood in the ice-cold water for the whole night as the guards watched him. The next morning the guards brought the *brahmin* back to the court. Akbar was amazed at how brave the *brahmin* was. He asked, "How did you manage to stand in the cold water all night? Didn't you feel cold?"

The *brahmin* said, "Yes, my lord, I was feeling

very cold but then I looked at the lamps that were glowing in the palace towers. I kept looking at them all night and that kept me warm."

When Akbar heard this he was very angry. He shouted at the *brahmin*, "How dare you? The lamps have kept you warm all night. That is cheating. You shall not get any gold." And he asked the guards to throw the *brahmin* out of the court.

The poor *brahmin* was very upset. He knew that the emperor had been unfair to him. But who could argue with an emperor? Sadly, he went back home. Now, Birbal was present at the court when this happened. He thought, "The emperor is being very unfair. I must tell him that, so that the *brahmin* receives the gold that he deserves." Birbal walked to Akbar and bowed respectfully. He said, "*Jahanpanah*, I am arranging a party for my friends. I would like to invite you and all the ministers. Please come to my house today evening for dinner."

Akbar was very happy to know this. In the evening, he along with the ministers reached Birbal's house. But when they saw Birbal in his courtyard, they were very surprised. Birbal was sitting near a small fire while the pot which should have been on the fire, was hanging high up on a branch of a tree.

Akbar asked Birbal, "What do you think you are doing?" Birbal said, "Your majesty, I am making delicious khichdi for all of us." This made the emperor laugh out loud. He said, "You fool, how do you think will the heat from the fire reach the khichdi if the pot is hung up so high on that branch?"

Birbal said, "Just the way the heat from the lamps of the palace towers reached the poor *brahmin* that day." Akbar stopped laughing. He had realized what Birbal was trying to say. Next day he called for the *brahmin* and gave him the thousand gold coins as he had promised. The *brahmin* thanked and blessed the emperor. Akbar looked at Birbal as Birbal smiled back.

Most Foolish Person

The emperor Akbar had many hobbies. He liked playing chess and flying kites. He also liked listening to stories of other lands. But his favorite hobby was collecting horses, good horses.

One day a horse dealer came to the palace. He had a team of horses to sell. The emperor came out and looked at the horses.

"They are very fine horses," said Akbar. "I'll buy them. Have you got any more?"

"No sir," said the dealer. "But if you give me some money, I will go to Afghanistan and buy some more."

Akbar gave the horse dealer two hundred gold coins for the team of horses, and two hundred gold coins to bring more horses from Afghanistan. He gave him the money but he did not ask him any questions. He did not ask what his name was, where he came from, or where he lived.

The horse dealer took the money and went away.

Many days passed but the horse dealer did not return. Akbar was growing impatient.

A few days later, Akbar asked Birbal to make a list of the ten biggest fools in India. Birbal made the list very quickly, and took it to the emperor. As Akbar began to read it he was first surprised, then very angry. Birbal had written Akbar's name at the very top of the list.

"What's this, Birbal?" the emperor shouted. "Why is my name at the top of the list?"

"*Jahanpanah*, it is because you are the biggest fool of all people," Birbal uttered.

"How dare you?" Akbar said, being very hurt by Birbal's words. Birbal was calm and continued, "Your majesty, you gave such a large sum of money to a stranger, and you didn't ask who he was or where he came from. Isn't that foolish?"

Akbar said, "What if the man returns with the horses?"

"Your majesty, if he returns with the horses, I'll remove your name from the top of the list, and write his name there instead," said Birbal.

Akbar realized he had indeed been foolish.

Most Beautiful Child

Once, Emperor Akbar declared in the court that his grandson was the most beautiful child in the whole land. He was very fond of his new born grandson. Akbar loved his grandson so much that after the child was born Akbar could hardly concentrate on his duties as the emperor. He would play with the child all day. This made the ministers worry.

So when Akbar said, his grandson was the most beautiful child in the land. Birbal said, "*Jahanpanah*, please do not be offended. The prince is no doubt a beautiful child but I think there are children more beautiful than him."

Akbar was very angry when he heard this. He said, "How can you say that? I order all the ministers to bring a child they think is the most beautiful. If those children are more beautiful than my grandson, I would agree with what Birbal has said."

So the next day each minister brought a child to the court. But Birbal was nowhere to be seen. Then after some time Birbal came to the court. He was drenched with sweat. Akbar asked, "Where is the child you said was more beautiful than my grandson?" Birbal said, "Your majesty, I tried to bring the child to the court but his mother wouldn't let me. If you can dress like a commoner we can go to see the child."

Akbar and some of his ministers dressed as commoners and went with Birbal to see the child. After a long walk they came to a hut. A child was playing on a heap of dirt outside the hut. He was covered with dirt. One of its eyes was smaller than the other and streams of water ran from its nose. Akbar said to Birbal, "You think this child is more beautiful than the prince? He is so ugly!"

But as Akbar said it, the child's mother came out of the hut. She was very angry at the men who were standing and looking at the child. She said, "Who are you? How dare you call my son ugly. Get out of here!" And she picked up the child, wiped his face with the end of her *saree* and kissed him. She said to the boy, "Don't listen to these men darling, you are the most beautiful child in the land." She them took the little boy inside.

Akbar understood what Birbal wanted to say. He said, "Every child is the most beautiful in the land for their parents." Birbal smiled and said, "And at times for their grandparents."

Strange Invitation

Emperor Akbar would often lose his temper with Birbal. On one such occasion, he asked Birbal to leave the royal court and never return. This hurt Birbal very much and he left the city one night without letting anyone know.

After a few days, Akbar began to miss Birbal very much. He realized he had been a little too harsh on poor Birbal. So the emperor sent his messengers to look for Birbal in the neighbouring towns and cities. But alas! None of the messengers could find Birbal.

Akbar thought, "Birbal must have disguised himself. That is why the messengers have not been able to find him. There has to be some other way of finding out where Birbal is hiding."

Akbar ordered his ministers to send invitation cards to all the kings of the city. The invitation card was very strange for it and

read, "The sea of my kingdom wants to get married. All the rivers of your kingdom are invited. Please send them as early as possible as the marriage will take place next week."

All the kings who received the invitation were very puzzled. They did not know what to write in reply. So they decided not to reply to the invitation and pretend as if they had not received it. But after some days, Emperor Akbar received a reply from one of the kings. It said, "Thank you very much for your kind invitation. We shall be happy to send our rivers for the wedding but they have requested that your sea must come halfway to receive them."

Akbar laughed very hard for a long time when he read the reply. Then with his guards, he went to the city of the king to request Birbal to return. Akbar had guessed it right. Indeed, Birbal was living with the king who had sent the reply. Akbar was very happy when he found Birbal. He said, "I knew only you could have written a fitting reply to my invitation. I am really sorry for hurting you. Please come back to my court."

Birbal too was glad to see that the emperor himself had come to take him back. He bade farewell to the king and left the city with Akbar.

Sweet Punishment

One day, Akbar came to court in a very thoughtful mood. He looked around at all his ministers present at the court and said, "My dear ministers, tell me, what punishment should I give to the one who dares to pull my beard?"

The court was alarmed at such a strange question. Everyone began to discuss amongst themselves about how usual the offence was. Who would dare to pull the emperor's beard?

One of the minsters said, "My lord, someone who dares to do such a deed must have his hands chopped off!"

Another minister said, "Yes, my lord, he deserves nothing less than death."

Then another rose and said, "Your majesty must punish such an evil-doer with life imprisonment. He should be thrown in the dungeons with the rats!"

The ideas for a fitting punishment came pouring in. The ministers got more and more creative as they went on discussing. Akbar was listening to all of them with great relish. Finally, he turned to Birbal and said, "Why dear Birbal, why are you so quite? What do you think should be a fitting punishment for the one who dares to pull my beard?"

Birbal rose and bowed to the emperor. Then he said, "Your majesty, he should be showered with kisses and hugs and given lots of sweets to eat."

At this the court broke out into a surprise, again. A minister said, "My lord, it is nothing less than a crime to pull the emperor's beard and Birbal wants the person to be given sweets?" Akbar was smiling. He asked Birbal, "Why do you think it is a fitting punishment?" Birbal replied, "My lord, who else will dare to pull your beard but your own grand children?"

Birbal was right. That morning, when the emperor was playing with his grandson, he had mischievously pulled his grandfather's beard. Akbar had thought it was a good idea to test his ministers, so he had put the strange question to them.

Only Birbal had been able to answer the question correctly. Akbar presented Birbal with a bag of gold for his intelligent thought.